Replacement costs will be
billed after 42 days overdue.

SUPER SANDCASTLE
Creature Features

What Has Horns?

Mary Elizabeth Salzmann

ABDO
Publishing Company

Published by ABDO Publishing Company, 8000 West 78th Street, Edina, Minnesota 55439. Copyright © 2008 by Abdo Consulting Group, Inc. International copyrights reserved in all countries. No part of this book may be reproduced in any form without written permission from the publisher. Super SandCastle™ is a trademark and logo of ABDO Publishing Company.

Printed in the United States.

Credits

Editor: Pam Price

Content Developer: Nancy Tuminelly

Cover and Interior Design and Production: Mighty Media

Photo Credits: Digital Vision, iStockphoto (JamesSapp), Peter Arnold (John Cancalosi), Shutterstock, Steve Wewerka

Library of Congress Cataloging-in-Publication Data

Salzmann, Mary Elizabeth, 1968-

 What has horns? / Mary Elizabeth Salzmann.

   p. cm. -- (Creature features)

 ISBN 978-1-59928-868-0

 1. Horns--Juvenile literature. 2. Ungulates--Juvenile literature. I. Title.

 QL942.S25 2007

 591.47--dc22

                2007003719

Super SandCastle™ books are created by a team of professional educators, reading specialists, and content developers around five essential components—phonemic awareness, phonics, vocabulary, text comprehension, and fluency—to assist young readers as they develop reading skills and strategies and increase their general knowledge. All books are written, reviewed, and leveled for guided reading, early reading intervention, and Accelerated Reader® programs for use in shared, guided, and independent reading and writing activities to support a balanced approach to literacy instruction.

About SUPER SANDCASTLE™

Bigger Books for Emerging Readers
Grades PreK–3

Created for library, classroom, and at-home use, Super SandCastle™ books support and engage young readers as they develop and build literacy skills and will increase their general knowledge about the world around them. Super SandCastle™ books are part of SandCastle™, the leading PreK–3 imprint for emerging and beginning readers. Super SandCastle™ features a larger trim size for more reading fun.

Let Us Know
Super SandCastle™ would like to hear your stories about reading this book. What was your favorite page? Was there something hard that you needed help with? Share the ups and downs of learning to read. We want to hear from you! Send us an e-mail.

sandcastle@abdopublishing.com

Contact us for a complete list of SandCastle™, Super SandCastle™, and other nonfiction and fiction titles from ABDO Publishing Company.

www.abdopublishing.com • 8000 West 78th Street Edina, MN 55439 • 800-800-1312 • 952-831-1632 fax

Horns grow on the heads of some creatures.
Horns come in many shapes and sizes.

Cows have horns.

Horns grow out of an animal's skull.
True horns are hollow. They are
made of bone covered with a layer
of keratin.

Bison have horns.

Animals use their horns to fight and to protect themselves. They also use their horns to root in the ground or to strip bark from trees.

Ibex have horns.

Ibex are a kind of goat. Their horns are long and curved, with ridges on the front. Male ibex have much larger horns than female ibex.

Horned lizards have horns.

The horns on a horned lizard's head
are true horns. The spines on a
horned lizard's body look like horns,
but they are modified scales.

Kudu have horns.

Kudu are a kind of antelope. Of all the horned animals, they have the longest horns.

Rams have horns.

Rams are male sheep. Their horns can be very curly.

Mountain goats have horns.

Mountain goat horns are black and very sharp. Their horns are usually less than a foot long.

Deer have horns.

Deer horns are called antlers. Unlike true horns, antlers fall off and regrow each year.

Rhinoceroses have horns.

Rhino horns are also not true horns. They grow out of the skin on their noses rather than their skulls. They are made entirely of keratin.

What would you do if you had horns?

MORE CREATURES
THAT HAVE HORNS

bull

pronghorn

goat

impala

yak

GLOSSARY

creature - a living being, especially an animal or an insect.

curve - to bend smoothly without any sharp angles.

keratin - a fibrous protein found in hair, feathers, hooves, claws, and horns.

protect - to guard someone or something from harm or danger.

reptile - a cold-blooded animal, such as a snake, turtle, or alligator, that moves on its belly or on very short legs.

ridge - a narrow, raised area on the surface of something.

root - to search for something.

skull - the bones that protect the brain and form the face.

usually - commonly or normally.